Buck Wilder's Adventures

Book #2

THE *WORK BEES* GO ON *STRIKE*

D1044338

Other Buck Wilder Books

Buck Wilder's Adventures Chapter Books

Buck Wilder's Animal Wisdom
Buck Wilder's Small Fry Fishing Guide
Buck Wilder's Small Twig Hiking and Camping Guide
Buck Wilder's Little Skipper Boating Guide

...and more to come...

Buck Wilder's Animal Adventures #2: The Work Bees Go on Strike
Written by Timothy R. Smith

Copyright 2007 Timothy R. Smith

Library of Congress Cataloging-in-Publication Data

Smith, Timothy R.

Buck Wilder's Adventures #2
The Work Bees Go on Strike
Summary: Buck Wilder® and friends work to solve why the bees are on strike and refusing to work.

ISBN 978-0-9643793-9-8

Fiction
10 9 8 7 6 5 4

Buck Wilder Adventures
4160 M-72 East
Williamsburg, MI 49690

www.buckwilder.com

"You never take more than your share."
B.W.

THE WORK BEES GO ON STRIKE

CHAPTERS

Introduction

You will need this introduction in case you don't know who Buck Wilder is, or if you have never met his family of friends, or if you do not know where he lives. A longer introduction is in Buck Wilder's first adventure, *Who Stole the Animal Poop?*.

Way back in the deep woods in the middle of the forest is this really neat tree house. Not a normal tree house–this tree house is really big. It is a real house in the trees and it looks kind of like this:

In this tree house lives a really nice man. He is tall, older looking, and has a lot of wisdom. He is kind, gentle, and he knows a lot about nature. His name is Buck Wilder and he looks kind of like this:

I love the outdoors.

Buck has a whole bunch of friends. They live in the woods around him. They are his good animal friends. They respect Buck's wisdom and they like to visit him as often as possible. They all get along great. This is how they kind of look:

Buck Wilder's best friend and most trusted companion is Rascal Raccoon. He is not just an ordinary raccoon, he is a <u>rascal</u> raccoon and he's a great detective. He knows all of the animals in the woods and he loves to solve mysteries.

He looks kind of like this:

Now for the story. It is a good one because it's a Buck Wilder adventure story. It is the story about why...
'the

work

bees

went

on

strike!'

TURN
THE PAGE
and
let's get started

CHAPTER 1

IN THE TREE HOUSE

It all started like this. Buck Wilder and his good friend Rascal Raccoon were having just a normal day in the tree house, matching socks, taking out the trash, and making peanut butter and jelly sandwiches when all of a sudden the bell rang.

The bell rings anytime someone visits Buck in his treehouse. Buck has many visitors, his animal friends, who often come to visit, stopping in for lunch with the hope there might be an extra peanut butter and jelly sandwich. The bell ringing meant that Rascal needed to lower the ladder to let them in.

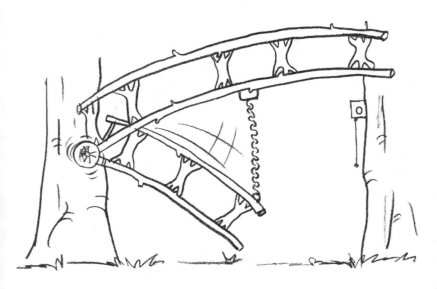

This day was different though. On this day, Lucy the Robin and her twin sister Sadie came to visit Buck with a real problem in the woods–they needed Buck's help.

CHAPTER 2

COME ON UP

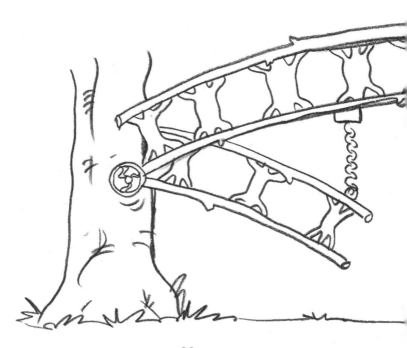

"Hello down there," yelled Rascal. "Come on up."

Lucy the Robin and her twin sister Sadie had pulled the chain to ring the bell just to be polite.

They did not need the ladder. They just flew up. A few beats of their wings and a little hop and there they were. "Hi, Buck," said Lucy.

"How goes it, Rascal?" said Sadie.

"Just great!" replied Rascal. "All of my socks matched!"

"Well, hello, Lucy and Sadie," said Buck. "What brings me such honor that the twin robin sisters would come visit me? Glad you are here. I've been fishing a lot lately and have some extra worms in the refrigerator. Want to take some back to the youngin's?" You see, robins always have youngin's, baby chicks, to feed. They seem to spend their whole lives building nests, laying small, blue eggs, and hatching a bunch of mouths to feed. And what baby robins like to eat most is worms…and Buck knew that.

"Thanks, Buck," they said. "That's very nice of you to ask, but we are here for a bigger reason. We have a major problem in the woods and we need your help."

"What is it?" said Buck. Rascal sat up on the edge of his chair to listen closely.

Sadie spoke first. "It is serious, Buck. Lucy and I have stopped singing in the woods. We can't sing together anymore. We can't carry a tune. We don't have any harmony and we have just stopped singing. And it is not just us–all the birds have stopped!"

"Oh my gosh," said Buck. "That is big. What's the matter–everybody have colds, cough, catch the flu? What is it?"

"It is the rhythm of our songs, our beat: there's no music in the woods. We always sing to the rhythm of bees buzzing in the air. You know, their

I'm going to listen close.

constant buzzing back and forth gives us the rhythm to sing our songs to. We just can't sing without them!"

Then Lucy spoke up, "The problem is this, Buck: the bees have stopped buzzing. They are not flying. There is not any music in the woods!"

CHAPTER 3

THIS IS SERIOUS

"Wow, this is serious," said Buck. "We have to have singing! Thanks for telling me. I'll see if I can help. Rascal, again, this is a job for you. You know your way around the woods and all of the animals are your friends. Go out there and find out what is going on. Find out why there isn't any buzzing in the air. Find out why the bees aren't flying and find out where they are." So off went Rascal with Lucy and Sadie joining him.

"Wow, you were right," said Rascal. "I've never heard the woods so quiet. There is very little sound in the air. You can only hear the wind pushing the leaves around. The buzzing is gone. The flowers are very still and not smiling. The fruit trees are sad and their limbs are hanging down.

"Let's go over to the beehive and see what is going on." So off they went.

CHAPTER 4

THE BEEHIVE

The beehive is where the bees both work and live. A typical beehive will have as many as 40,000 to 50,000 bees working and living together. That is a big family! The bees share their work responsibilities being workers, transporters, builders, food processors, and guards. The one female that rules over the whole place is the Queen Bee.

She lays up to 2,000 eggs a day, and whatever she wants, she gets. She's the Queen! They are very organized, smart little creatures that have survived on our planet for over forty million years.

When Rascal, Lucy, and Sadie arrived at the beehive they were astonished at what they saw. Marching around the beehive was a long line of worker bees carrying written signs and chanting a tune, "♪ Work all day, sleep all night, someone help us with our plight! ♪"

Their signs said things like 'unfair work conditions,' 'we can't keep up,' and 'overworked.' They were very upset and not happy. They had gone on strike. They refused to work until

their working conditions had improved.
"Wow," said Rascal. "I've never seen
anything like this before."

"I didn't know insects would go on strike!" said Lucy.

"I didn't know that bees could march in a line. They look like little soldiers," said Sadie

"I think it's time we report back to Buck," Rascal said. So back to the tree house they went.

CHAPTER 5

THIS IS QUITE A PROBLEM

Rascal ran like a bullet to tell Buck what he had found out. As soon as the three arrived back at the tree house Rascal started to blurt out everything. "Buck, they are marching, they are in a row, they are carrying signs, they are…"

"Whoa, slow down, Rascal," said Buck. "Tell me everything and keep it in order, please." So Rascal took a deep breath and started with what he heard–or did not hear–in the woods: the lack of buzzing. Then he explained about the beehive and what he learned from the bees. He told Buck everything he found out and Lucy and Sadie backed it all up with what they saw. Buck listened very carefully and then said, "Very interesting. This is quite a problem. They were actually holding signs?"

"Yup," said Rascal.

Buck thought for a moment and then said, "Here is what we do. If possible, I would like a meeting with Queen Mary, the Queen of the Beehive. She will know exactly what is going on."

"Buck, I don't think anyone has seen Queen Mary in over a year or so! She's the Queen of the whole place and they never let her out of the hive."

"I know, Rascal. I'll go to the hive and meet with her if she will come out on her balcony. See if you can arrange a meeting."

"Okay," said Rascal and off he went. Lucy and Sadie each said goodbye, taking a few worms with them.

Thanks for all the help and I like your new shoes!

Thanks for noticing!

I hope you are singing soon!

Good luck, Buck!

CHAPTER 6

BACK TO THE HIVE

When Rascal got to the hive he found nothing had changed. The sun was still up, but the bees still were not buzzing. They were still marching and holding signs. The first bee that Rascal met was the bee that guarded the front door of the hive, Izzy Bee.

"Hi, Izzy Bee," said Rascal.

"Hi, Rascal. See all the action around here?" responded Izzy. "There is a lot going on. I don't know exactly what is happening, but I know the worker bees are very upset and our honey production has come to a standstill."

"That's why I'm here, Izzy. Do you think you can arrange a meeting with Queen Mary and Buck Wilder? How about at daybreak tomorrow, when the black and white of night leaves and the color of the day appears, and Queen Mary can come to her balcony?"

"No one from the outside ever gets to see the Queen Bee, but I'll ask." Izzy put another bee as the door guard and went inside. A few moments later, out she came with a surprised look on her face. "I don't believe it, Rascal. The Queen said to me, 'It's been a long time since I've seen Buck Wilder. I'd love to see him. I bet he looks older. Tomorrow, daybreak, I'll be on my balcony.'"

CHAPTER 7

MEETING THE QUEEN

The next morning, just as the day breaks, when the black and white leaves and the color of the day appears, Buck and Rascal were standing outside the balcony to the Queen's room. Buck was holding a bunch of freshly picked wildflowers and had a big smile on his face. A few minutes after their arrival out walked the Queen herself surrounded by six personal guards.

"Good morning, Queen Mary," said Buck. "I brought you a bouquet of freshly picked wildflowers. I thought you might enjoy them."

"A very good morning to you Buck, and to you, Rascal," replied the Queen. "Buck, no one has brought me flowers for a very long time. You are very thoughtful."

"My pleasure, Queen Mary. Thank you for seeing us."

"What may I help you with today? What's going on?"

"That's just what I wanted to ask you–what's going on? Why are the worker bees on strike and can I be of any help?"

"Oh, we have a problem in the hive. A big one! We can't keep up with the honey demand. Our worker bees are overworked, tired, and need a rest–so they've gone on strike. They won't work anymore. They want better working conditions and I don't blame them. Our honey is going out faster then we can produce it and we don't know why. It is going to have to stop or there won't be any honey at all!"

"Hmmmm," muttered Buck thoughtfully. "That would be a big problem and a problem for everything that is connected with it too! Can I help?"

"Yes!" said Queen Mary. "We'll take all the help we can get. Oh, I love these fresh flowers. They smell so great. That is so very nice of you. I don't get out much anymore and no one brings me fresh flowers. They keep me busy running this place and I'm always stocking the nursery."

"I'd like to do this, if it's okay with you," said Buck. "Here is my plan. Rascal Raccoon is such a great detective and he's really good at getting into things and finding out what is going on in the woods. He's quiet and sees well in the dark. I'm going to ask him to climb a nearby tree, keep an eye on the place, and find out what he can. It may take him a day or two, but I think it might help."

"Good idea," said Queen Mary. "Thanks for the help. I have to get back to the hive and lay more eggs. Let me know what you find out." Queen Mary went back into her hive, surrounded by all the guard bees.

"Rascal, here's what I'd like you to do. Pick out a good tree, climb it, and get yourself into a high spot. Hide for a while and see what you can find out. Get one of your animal friends to join you to keep you company. Two sets of eyes are better than one."

"Okay, Buck," said Rascal and off he went. Buck headed for home.

CHAPTER 8

RASCAL AND MAURY

Rascal decided to visit his friend Maury the Moose and asked for his help in 'staking out' the hive.

I'd love a twig sandwich!

"Be glad to," said Maury, "as long as I have some fresh leaves and tree tops to chew on. I love to stay up late, eat under the stars, and sleep late in the morning. I can be really quiet if you want. Count on me." So off went Rascal and Maury to 'stake out' the hive.

"Let's hide behind that tree," Rascal said when they arrived. "It has plenty of fresh leaves on it and it would be fun for me to sit up in your antlers. That way we could whisper quietly to each other. You're as strong as a bull and I'm sure you could hold me with no problem."

"Fun," replied Maury.

Quietly Rascal and Maury hid

behind a tree until the sun went down and the color of the day left and the dark came in. Everything got really quiet. Most of the forest animals were asleep and the bees were quietly sleeping in their hive. Off in the distance you could even hear Buck snoring in his tree house. The place was so quiet that it didn't take long for Rascal and Maury to also fall sound asleep!

Sometime after midnight Rascal was awakened by what sounded like buckets and handles clinking together in the dark. He quietly gave Maury a poke and whispered in his ear, "Maury, wake up! Open your eyes and take a good look over at the beehive and tell me if you see what I see."

"Looks to me," whispered Maury, "like two bears, young cubs, with buckets under the honey spigot."

"Looks like that to me too," said Rascal. In a matter of minutes, the bears were gone.

"Wow, that was fast. Good thing we were both awake."

CLOSED FOR THE NIGHT!

"Yeah," said Rascal yawning. "I'm tired."

"Me too," said Maury. "Let's go back to sleep and see Buck in the morning and tell him what we saw."

"Good idea," said Rascal rubbing his eyes, and again, in no time, they were both sound asleep.

CHAPTER 9

THE NEXT MORNING

When morning came Rascal and Maury were back in the tree house. "Good morning, Maury," said Buck. "Would you like a fresh bowl of twigs and leaves for breakfast? Maybe with a little milk on them? How about you, Rascal? Do you want some cereal?"

"Sounds great," they both responded. "It's been a long night, and we're hungry." As soon as they finished eating Buck asked what they had found out. So Rascal and Maury explained what they saw and what happened.

"Hmmm," muttered Buck, as he usually does when he's listening closely. "I think we need to make a visit to the Bear den and ask a few questions." Maury said goodbye to head back to the woods for his morning nap and Buck and Rascal took off for the Bear's den.

CHAPTER 10

BORIS AND BEATRICE BEAR

Bears like to live in a den. Sometimes a bear den is an old cave or a big hole in the side of a hill–a big place where they can raise the whole family. Bears are big animals and need a lot of room, especially in the winter when they stay inside for months. Boris and Beatrice Bear lived down by the stream in a dug out old cave section where their parents had lived before them and their parents before that. It was an old home, but it worked great for the Bear's. They also had two sons, Jer Bear and Alex Bear, who lived with them. Like normal bear cubs they liked to play, get into mischief, and were always wrestling with each other. As Buck and Rascal approached the bear den, Buck started to sing a little jingle to let the Bear's know that someone was coming into their territory. "♪ Take me out to the ball game, take me out to the crowd. Buy me some peanuts and cracker jacks, I don't care if I ever come back ♪," Buck always liked baseball. Bears, like most animals, never like to be surprised. They get angry about surprises.

"Yo ho, Boris and Beatrice, it's Buck Wilder and Rascal Raccoon coming for a visit," yelled Buck as they came closer to the bear den. At the entrance to the den stood Boris and Beatrice Bear.

"Hello, Buck. Hello, Rascal," said Boris Bear. "We could hear you coming through the woods. What a nice surprise."

"Beautiful day," said Buck. "Good morning. Rascal and I have come for a short visit and we brought you a hat full of freshly picked blueberries that we just picked along the trail through the woods." Bears love blueberries. It is one of their most favorite foods and they can never eat enough of them because a bear's appetite is so big.

"Thank you, Buck. Thank you, Rascal. That is very generous and what a treat! We'll save these for a late night snack. Come on in."

Inside the den everything was clean, picked up, and orderly just like what you would expect. Buck spoke up first. "Are your boys around? Do you think we could talk to them for a minute?"

"Uh oh, what did they do?" said Beatrice Bear. "I love those boys, but they've been getting into a little trouble lately. You know young bear cubs. They want their independence, and then they get a little mischievous, but still expect us to take care of them. They are starting to drive us nuts! Every week it's something new. I'm sure they're home. They're probably in their room, in bed, sound asleep. They do sleep a lot."

CHAPTER 11

GOOD MORNING, BOYS

Boris and Beatrice Bear, along with Buck and Rascal, went down the hall to the boys' room, opened their bedroom door and gave a quiet "Good morning, boys. Time to get up!"

Their room was a mess. There were clothes all over the place, dirty plates, dried-up cups . . . you couldn't even see the floor. "Boys, sit up and say hello to our morning visitors. They've come to see you," said Beatrice Bear. Both boys sat up in bed, rubbed their eyes, gave a morning stretch, looked at Buck and said, "Good morning, sir" and to Rascal it was, "Hi, Rascal."

"Boys, we are having a slight problem in the woods and I think those honey buckets next to your bed have something to do with it," Buck said.

"Oops," said Jer Bear, like he just had gotten caught. "Ah – oo – ah – a." He was at a loss for words. Alex sat quiet.

"Boys? Explain," Boris Bear said in a deep, father-type voice he only used when he meant no fooling around.

"Dad," Alex said, looking up from studying his toes, "we can't help it. You know how honey is our favorite treat and how we all love it." At that moment Jer Bear and Alex jumped from their beds, put their hands in the air, started dancing in a circle singing, "♪ Honey in the morning, honey in the evening, honey at suppertime—be my little honey and I'll love you all the time.♪"

"Stop!" yelled Boris Bear. And they did.

"Oh, teenagers," said Mama Bear shaking her head and looking at the mess all over the floor.

"What's going on?" said Boris Bear.

Jer Bear, who now had enough time to figure out what to say, explained, "Dad, sometimes at night, and I know we stay up too late, we get hungry and we don't want to make noise in the kitchen that might wake you up. We know that would make you angry, Dad. So, we sneak out our bedroom window, tip-toe over to the beehive, and get a late night snack. Just a little extra honey to hold us over until the morning. We mean no harm," shrugging his shoulders. "Have we caused a problem?"

"Boys, first you're in trouble because you are sneaking out of the house," their father said. "That's an absolute no. Second, you don't go in and out of your bedroom window, and third, you don't go out at night without us knowing where you are. And last, you're not going for a snack. Those are buckets you're taking."

"Oh," muttered both Alex and Jer as their shoulders dropped down and they looked at their feet. "Sorry, Dad."

"Boys," said Buck, "I'm sure you never realized it, but your late night bucket-o-honey snacks are causing quite a problem in the forest." Both boys looked up to meet Buck's eyes. "You see," continued Buck, "you are taking more than your share of honey and it's got the bees all upset. They can't make enough honey to feed your

appetites. The bees are worn out, tired–
they are refusing to work anymore.
They've gone on strike. And that's a
real problem because without the bees
working we are in danger of having no
fruit this year, a lack of flowers, and
flower seeds. You know how the bees
step on all of the flowers while buzzin'
around, and their feet spread the pollen
around pollinating the flowers for next
year's crop. If they're not buzzin',
they're not pollinating!"

"And," spoke up Beatrice Bear,
"that means no blueberries next year
and no blueberry jam!"

"Oh," said Alex still looking at
his feet.

"And, there's no music in the air,"

continued Buck. "The birds and the bees aren't performing together. It's stone quiet out there."

"Wow, we had no idea. I feel so bad," said Jer Bear.

"Me too," said Alex.

"We won't do it anymore, promise," said both Bear boys. "And no more sneaking out the window Dad…and we'll always tell you where we are going."

"Good," said Buck. "I know you meant no harm, but I think it would be a good idea if you went over to the beehive to apologize. That's the proper thing to do."

"What if they get mad and sting us?" asked Jer Bear.

"That they might," said Buck, "but you'll have to face the consequences."

"I think we'll go along with them," said Boris Bear, "just to smooth things out."

CHAPTER 12

THE APOLOGY

So off they went to the beehive. Upon their arrival they were met by Izzy Bee, the head guard bee, and a whole bunch of bees carrying signs. It was not a happy situation. The bear cubs explained and apologized.

"That is okay, boys. Thank you for admitting your mistake and telling us," said Izzy Bee. "And please tell the Queen we are sorry too."

"I will," said Izzy.

The presence of Buck and the parent bears helped a lot with the bees not being too upset. Some of them even spoke up and said they also had teenagers in the hive and understood. It looked like no one was going to get stung today! Jer and Alex promised to never take more than their share again and offered to do something nice for the bees to help make amends. Maybe cut the grass around the hive, knock down any tree branches in their way, hand dig them a swimming pool, or whatever the bees would like. "Nothing for now," said Izzy. "But thanks. We appreciate the thought."

After that the bears returned home and Buck and Rascal headed back to their quiet tree house and the woods went back to normal. The work bees went back to work, the flowers got pollinated, honey production came

back to normal and there was music in the air again. They even heard Sadie and Lucy singing again.

CHAPTER 13

BACK AT THE TREE HOUSE

It didn't take long for Rascal to get back into his normal routine of catching (and releasing) fish in Buck's aquarium, eating peanut butter and jelly sandwiches, and taking long afternoon naps.

Buck got back into his favorite thing to do–fishing. Buck just loves to fish, anytime, anyhow, anywhere.

For a long time everything continued normal and easy until one day Maury the Moose came to the tree house with a really big problem in the woods. The ants had gone and dug a hole all the way to China and they had started speaking Chinese! That's an adventure story in Buck's next book– 'The Ants Dig to China.' See you there!

SECRET MESSAGE DECODING PAGE

Hidden in this book is a secret Buck Wilder message. You need to figure it out. Hidden in many of the drawings are letters that, when put together, make up a statement, a Buck Wilder statement. Your job is to find those letters and always remember the message – it's important.

DO NOT write in this book if it's from the library, your classroom, or borrowed from someone.

If you need help finding the hidden letters turn the page.

You'll need these words in life!

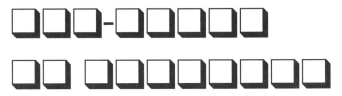

18 letters make up 3 words.

The secret letters are hidden on the
following pages in this order…

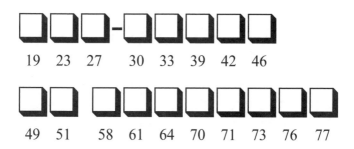

19 23 27   30 33 39 42 46

49 51   58 61 64 70 71 73 76 77

18 letters make up 3 words.

Remember – Don't Write in this Book!

Buck Wilder